1

S.

2

Nïpper McFee

In Trouble with PC Poodle

Get

Plea:
You
Or b'

For Lewis
R.I.

For Isaac
M.W.

Reading Consultant: Prue Goodwin, Lecturer in literacy and children's books

ORCHARD BOOKS
338 Euston Road, London NW1 3BH
Orchard Books Australia
Hachette Children's Books
Level 17/207 Kent Street, Sydney NSW 2000

First published in 2011 by Orchard Books

Text © Rose Impey 2011
Illustrations © Melanie Williamson 2011

The rights of Rose Impey to be identified as the author and
Melanie Williamson to be identified as the illustrator of this work
have been asserted by them in accordance with the
Copyright, Designs and Patents Act, 1988.

ISBN 978 1 40830 223 1 (hardback)
ISBN 978 1 40830 231 6 (paperback)

1 3 5 7 9 10 8 6 4 2 (hardback)
1 3 5 7 9 10 8 6 4 2 (paperback)

Printed in China

Orchard Books is a division of Hachette Children's Books,
an Hachette UK company.

www.hachette.co.uk

Nipper McfFee

In Trouble with PC Poodle

Written by ROSE IMPEY
Illustrated by MELANIE WILLIAMSON

ORCHARD BOOKS

Nipper McFee might have seen trouble coming – if only he had stopped to look.

But, as usual, Nipper was having far too much fun with his friends, Will and Lil. They were fighting their enemies – the basement rats.

Get Nipper!

Sometimes, other people got caught
in the crossfire.
Today, Mrs Lulu Lamb was just
coming out of Mr Mewler's shop . . .

CORNER SHOP

. . . when the tomatoes landed.

"You have to do something
about those young hoodlums!"
Mrs Lulu Lamb told PC Poodle.

PC Poodle shone his torch at
Nipper and his friends.

"You had better find somewhere else
to play," he warned them, "or
you'll be in *big* trouble with me."

9

"But where else can we play?" said Will. "We need a place of our own," said Lil. "A den!" suggested Nipper. And he knew just the place. "But it has to be a secret," he whispered. "We don't want the *R-A-T-S* to find out."

Will and Lil looked over their shoulders and nodded.

But the *R-A-T-S* were just round the corner and earwigging as usual.

They knew something was
going on. And whatever it was . . .
they weren't going to be left out.

Not far away was a big, old factory.
It had been closed down for years.
But Nipper knew how to get
in – through an open window.

Inside the factory, it was very dark and dusty. They were all feeling a little nervous, but no one wanted to look like a scaredy-cat.

"I hope it's not haunted," giggled Lil.

Haunted?

Nooooo!

They found steep staircases
to slide down . . .

and big cupboards
to hide in . . .

and long conveyer belts
to play skittles on.

They were having lots of fun
when suddenly they heard doors
b-b-banging and stairs *c-c-creaking.*
It sounded as if the place really
was *h-h-haunted*!

The three friends ran out of the
factory so fast you might have
thought their tails were on fire.

And the minute they left, *trouble* moved in. The rats hung out of the windows laughing.

"We got Nipper!" they squealed.

"Now we've got the den!"

Nipper and his friends were furious.
They wanted to get their den back
from those pesky rats. But how?
For once Nipper didn't have a plan.

As they walked along the street, they saw something lying on the ground. It was a torch.
It was PC Poodle's torch.

Now Nipper had a plan.

Inside the factory the rats were playing cards. It was so dark, they could hardly see the spots.

They were still laughing about
how they had fooled Nipper and
his friends.

"We really fixed those felines,"
they squealed.
"What a gang of scaredy-cats!"

Will and Lil wanted to rush out and grab those rats, but Nipper whispered, "Wait."

He would soon put the cats among the rats – but not yet.

Nipper and Will crept up
the stairs while Lil waited at
the bottom – with the torch.

When Nipper gave the signal, Lil turned on the torch. Then Nipper and Will gave the most monstrous roars. "Grrrr! R-raaa!" they roared.

The rats didn't see Nipper and
Will. They only saw two *enormous*
shadows!

The rats were terrified!

They ran in all directions, trying
to escape. Most of them jumped
through the windows.
They fell down,

down,

down . . .

. . . right into PC Poodle's hands. "Breaking and entering is a very serious crime," he said as he led the rats away.

"And so is messing with Nipper," added Nipper.

But over the next week Nipper and his friends were *so* bored.

They were really glad when the rats came back – and the fun could start again.

Get Nipper!

ROSE IMPEY ✳ MELANIE WILLIAMSON

In Trouble with Great Aunt Twitter   978 1 40830 224 8

In Trouble with Growler Grimes   978 1 40830 225 5

In Trouble with Bertie Barker   978 1 40830 226 2

In Trouble with Mrs Lulu Lamb   978 1 40830 227 9

In Trouble with Mrs McFee   978 1 40830 228 6

In Trouble with Primrose Paws   978 1 40830 229 3

In Trouble with Susie Soapsuds   978 1 40830 230 9

In Trouble with PC Poodle   978 1 40830 231 6

All priced at £4.99

Orchard Books are available from all good bookshops,
or can be ordered from our website: www.orchardbooks.co.uk,
or telephone 01235 827702, or fax 01235 827703.

Prices and availability are subject to change.